THERE ARE NO MOOSE IN MAINE

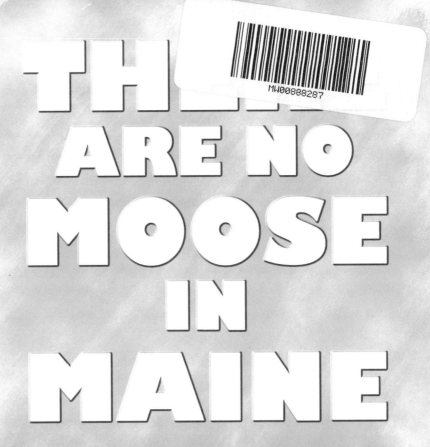

Written By
Joyce Jackson

Illustrated By
Shaun Stotyn

WARNING: Do not continue reading this book unless you are both curious and careful as reading it may result in unexpected sojourns or perilous adventure. The curious are already on the path of discovery but only the careful are wise enough to be fully prepared for the unexpected.

There Are No Moose in Maine

© 2019 Joyce R. Jackson

Screven and Allen Publishing
ISBN 978-1-7322923-3-8

Author Dedication

To Dr. David who "takes good care of people" including me and to my four children, Sarah, Rebekah, Jonathan and Emily who are both curious and careful and as such can expect to find their own adventures.

Illustrator Dedication

To my children, Cadence Mae and Ransom. May they grow up with the same sense of curiosity and adventure as the characters in this book.

Special acknowledgment for the inspiration of this story goes to Marilyn McClendon who demonstratively uttered the phrase, "There are no moose in Maine!" Marilyn encourages young people to, "Seek and you shall find." She has helped many along their journey. May you find your Moose Marilyn.

"There are no moose in Maine!" Maggie exclaimed. "We have bear and bats, fox, deer and wild cats but there are absolutely no moose in Maine."

Clyde chuckled, for he had seen a moose but wisely said, "Perhaps you should search to be certain that you haven't missed a moose."

"Missed a moose, hardly!" Maggie huffed. "And to prove this fact we shall start our quest where the first light of day reaches the United States. At dawn we climb **Cadillac Mountain**."

Clyde grinned, "Hooray!"

Beginning in the chill of early morning with stars twinkling themselves to sleep, Maggie and Clyde climbed towards Cadillac Mountain's peek. The first fingers of sunlight crept up from the ocean and stretched across the sky. **Acadia National Park** spread around them and Maggie felt sure she would spot a Maine moose from this perch, if there were such a thing.

Pulling out her spyglass she pointed it towards the bay of **Bar Harbor** scanning up coast to **West Quoddy Head**, then around to **Mars Hill Mountain**, next towards **Moose Head** and finally sweeping all the way around to **Portland**. There was even a little **black capped chickadee**, Maine's state bird, dancing in a **blueberry bush**.

With no Moose in sight Maggie was miffed. Heading back down Cadillac Mountain they stopped to search at **Blue Hill Summit** where Clyde pointed to a snowy owl circling above.

Further down **Thunder Hole** lived up to it's name kicking up a water spout and spraying Maggie and Clyde as they clung to the walkway railing.

Starving after their early morning moose hunt they stopped at **Molly-o's Breakfast** for scrumptious blueberry pancakes...

At **Otter Cliff** Maggie focused her spyglass on the trees above and the beautifully rounded boulders below. But no Moose appeared in her spyglass." Clyde decided the views were worth the trip.

...before heading to **Nubble Light at Cape Neddick.**

Maggie puckered her lips to blow dandelion seeds across the water, hoping at least one seed would make it to the lighthouse island. Clyde watched the dandelion puffs dance on the breeze and said, "Perhaps you should shed a little light on the matter."

Maggie replied dramatically waving her arm across the water view, "A little light indeed! **Maine has 65 lighthouses along 5000 miles of jagged coastland.**"

"Blue Hill Bay, Bear, Baker and Boone Island.

"Cobbossee and Doubling, Marshall and Maine, Pumpkin, Portland and Pemaquid," she sang.

Bird Coat, Burn Coat and Little Bird Island,

Wood Island, Goat Island, and Ram Island Ledge, Deer Island, Rock Island and West Quoddy Head.

Moose Peak, Whale Back and Squirrel Point, Nubble at Neddick,

Crabtree, Cuckold, Curtis and Grindle" she squeeked,

Spring Point, Fort Point and Owls Head, Egg Rock, Great Duck, Goose Rocks and Saddleback Ledge

Pirates roamed **Avery Rock** in olden days   Till in a Nor'easter it blew away. And let's not forget **Cape Elisabeth** the dear old lighthouse granny whose two lights shone like ancient eyes peering into the sea."

In honor of her lighthouse diddy, Clyde bowed low and offered her a **white pine cone** on a **white pine tree** branch, which are **Maine's state flower** and **Maine's state tree**. Maggie giggled at her own cleverness.

Maggie held up the white pine cone studying it seriously. "I don't think moose would hide in the **Desert of Maine** because they do love water.

I recall that the library has a book called, **'Hitty, Her First Hundred Years.'** If anyone would know where to find a moose in Maine it would be Hitty of **Cranberry Isles**." she said. So off they went to catch a **ferry boat** destined for Great Cranberry Island.

Clyde, being a good gentleman, held out his hand so Maggie could steady herself as she climbed aboard the ferry which bobbed up and down impatiently. She couldn't wait to meet the amazing Hitty and pressed her mind to remember details so she would be ready with a good conversation piece. Maggie remembered **Hitty's House** at **Preble Cove** and a friend named **Sammy Sanford** who sold vegetables in summer and ice in winter. She remembered that at first old Sammy had startled her but the old timer said that she was as safe as if she was in **God's Pocket** and with that they became fast friends telling of past adventures.

Maggie was so anxious to get to Hitty's house on **Great Cranberry Island** that she leapt out of the boat landing on the dock with a hollow thud.

Clyde followed her but choose to stay outside of the house tracing Hitty's name on the ground with his shoe. He realized that if written just so the letters of Hitty could be read right side up or up side down making the word an ambigram.

All too quickly Maggie reappeared looking positively mournful. "**Lobster** pots and **Penobscot** barnacles! Hitty has moved to Sturbridge, Massachusetts!" she cried. "Oh, I'm mortified, dejected, in utter angst and pain that I've dragged us all across Maine."

Maggie's shoulders slumped. Wandering away and into a patch of **cranberry** vines she gently lifted the leaves to peek at the cranberries still tiny and looking more like green peas. Maggie felt rather tiny and green herself.

Clyde allowed her a few moments of misery realizing that it is important to allow a little time for your feelings to run as long as you don't allow your feelings run you. Clearing his voice he said, "I'm reminded of our native son, **Henry Wadsworth Longfellow**'s words, 'The best thing one can do when it's raining is to let it rain'." For once Maggie was silent except for a little sniffling.

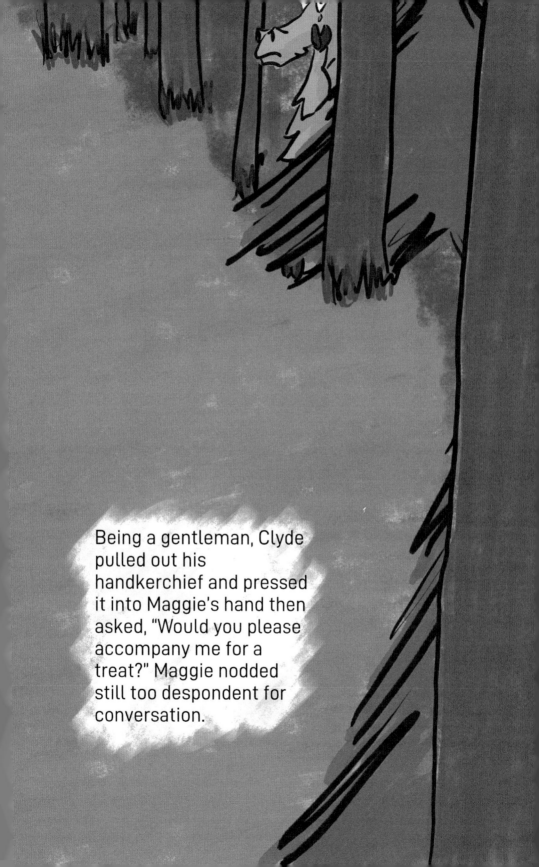

Being a gentleman, Clyde pulled out his handkerchief and pressed it into Maggie's hand then asked, "Would you please accompany me for a treat?" Maggie nodded still too despondent for conversation.

The trip was unnervingly quiet. To lift her spirits Clyde motioned to Augusta as they passed by saying, "Won't you give your regards to the governor?" Maggie leaned into the wind and shouted, "Best wishes to our benevolent governor and grand **Augusta** our fair **Capital**. We cannot stop today as we are on a quest."

With that Maggie sat back and eyed Clyde with curiosity asking, "Are we going for **Portland Lobster**? **The Holey Donut**? **Holey Cannoli**? **Wiscasset Treats**? **Red's Eats**? Clyde lifted a hand to quell the questions.

Soon a quaint confectionery, the **Len Libby Chocolatier**, came into view. "One simply cannot go wrong with good chocolate," Maggie announced as she opened the door. "Just look at the turtles and truffles, bear, lobster and moose tracks. I see almond butter crunch, nibbles, pretzels and the delectable Maine Chocolate Bah in stacks."

As Maggie turned she had such shock and delight that Clyde had to steady her for fear she would faint at the sight of **Lenny the Moose** staring straight at her. Standing eight feet tall and weighing 1700 pounds Lenny observed Maggie unblinking from his chocolate pond. "I would like to introduce you to Lenny, Maine's most famous moose," Clyde said.

A tiny giggle bubbled up, followed by a chuckle, then a chortle and finally a side aching roar of laughter rang from Maggie. Once again being a good gentleman, Clyde offered his handkerchief so Maggie could wipe away her tears of joy.

LENNY

As they sat nibbling at chocolate moose antlers and lobster tails Maggie grew thoughtful again and said. "I wonder if there are caribou in Caribou?"

The End.

Is Maggie a real person?

Maggie is a tribute to the magnificent Margaret Chase who married the distinguished statesman Clyde Smith. Both served the state of Maine honorably in the House of Representatives and Margaret Chase Smith became the first woman in the US to serve in both of the Houses of Congress. The wisdom of Clyde and determination of Margaret helped shape a stronger future for Maine.

Do the bold print words mean something?

All of the words in bold print are Maine treasures that one should experience and explore. There are many more wonderful Maine adventures to discover: beaches, villages, fairs and fishermen, covered bridges, scenic views, water falls, clam bakes, lobster and blueberries to name a few.

Does the author have to use such big words?
Absolutely! Many arguments could be transmogrified into mutually beneficial exchanges simply by enhancing vocabularies. Your own intelligence serves you best as it transforms your interaction with the world.

Do moose swim?
Is Lenny the moose real?
View the Lenny tab at lenlibby.com for some surprising facts.

Do you want to see a moose in person?
Not really, as they are huge and often have bad tempers. Moosehead Lake does have moose tours but take warning, moody moose are menacing.

You have persevered and triumphed in finishing this book. For this accomplishment you have earned the superlative adjective and title of, **positively perspicacious.**

Read-aloud assist pages are intended to help a reader before a group flow through the book without visually losing their place by flipping back and forth.

Pages 1-2 THERE ARE NO MOOSE IN MAINE

Written by Joyce Jackson

Illustrated by Shaun Stotyn

Pages 4-5 "There are no moose in Maine!" Maggie exclaimed. "We have bear and bats, fox, deer and wild cats but there are absolutely no moose in Maine." Clyde chuckled, for he had seen a moose but wisely said, "Perhaps you should search to be certain that you haven't missed a moose."

"Missed a moose, hardly!" Maggie huffed. "And to prove this fact we shall start our quest where the first light of day reaches the United States. At dawn we climb **Cadillac Mountain**."

Clyde grinned, "Hooray!"

Page 6-7 Beginning in the chill of early morning with stars twinkling themselves to sleep, Maggie and Clyde climbed towards Cadillac Mountain's peek. The first fingers of sunlight creptup from the ocean and stretched across the sky. **Acadia National Park** spread around them and Maggie felt sure she would spot a Maine moose from this perch, if there were such a thing.

Pulling out her spyglass she pointed it towards the bay of **Bar Harbor** scanning up coast to **West Quoddy Head**, then around to **Mars Hill Mountain**, next towards **Moose Head** and finally sweeping all the way around to **Portland**. There was even a little **black-capped chickadee**, **Maine's state bird**, dancing in a **blueberry bush**.

Page 8-9 With no Moose in sight Maggie was miffed. Heading back down Cadillac Mountain they stopped to search at **Blue Hill Summit** where Clyde pointed to a snowy owl circling above.Further down **Thunder Hole** lived up to it's name kicking up a water spout and spraying Maggie and Clyde as they clung to the walkway railing.

At **Otter Cliff** Maggie focused her spyglass on the trees above and the beautifully rounded boulders below. But no Moose appeared in her spyglass." Clyde decided the views were worth the trip.

Starving after their early morning moose hunt they stopped at **Molly-o's Breakfast** for scrumptious blueberry pancakes before heading to **Nubble Light at Cape Neddick**.

Page 10-11 Maggie puckered her lips to blow dandelion seeds across the water, hoping at least one seed would make it to the lighthouse island. Clyde watched the dandelion puffs dance on the breeze and said, "Perhaps you should shed a little light on the matter." Maggie replied dramatically waving her arm across the water view, "A little light indeed! **Maine has 65 lighthouses along 5000 miles of jagged coastland.**"

"**Cobbossee** and **Doubling, Marshall** and **Maine, Pumpkin, Portland** and **Pemaquid**," she sang. "**Blue Hill Bay, Bear, Baker** and **Boone Island. Bird Coat, Burn Coat** and **Little Bird Island, Crabtree, Cuckold, Curtis** and **Grindle**" she squeeked, "**Nubble at Neddick, Squirrel Point, Whale Back** and **Moose Peak, Wood Island, Goat Island,** and **Ram Island Ledge, Deer Island, Rock Island** and **West Quoddy Head. Spring Point, Fort Point** and **Owls Head, Egg Rock, Great Duck, Goose Rocks** and **Saddleback Ledge**.

Page 12-13 Pirates roamed **Avery Rock** in olden days Till in a Nor'easter it blew away. And let's not forget **Cape Elisabeth** the dear old lighthouse granny whose two lights shone like ancient eyes peering into the sea."

In honor of her lighthouse diddy, Clyde bowed low and offered her a **white pine cone** on a **white pine tree** branch, which are **Maine's state flower** and **Maine's state tree**. Maggie giggled at her own cleverness.

Page 14-15 Maggie held up the white pine cone studying it seriously. "I don't think moose would hide in the **Desert of Maine** because they do love water.

I recall that the library has a book called, '**Hitty, Her First Hundred Years**.' If anyone would know where to find a moose in Maine it would be Hitty of **Cranberry Isles**." she said. So off they went to catch a **ferry boat** destined for Great Cranberry Island.

Clyde, being a good gentleman, held out his hand so Maggie could steady herself as she climbed aboard the ferry which bobbed up and down impatiently. She couldn't wait to meet the amazing Hitty and pressed her mind to remember details so she would be ready with a good conversation piece. Maggie remembered **Hitty's House** at **Preble Cove** and a friend named **Sammy Sanford** who sold vegetables in summer and ice in winter. She remembered that at first old Sammy had startled her but the old timer said that she was as safe as if she was in **God's Pocket** and they became fast friends telling of past adventures.

Page 16-17 Maggie was so anxious to get to Hitty's house on **Great Cranberry Island** that she leapt out of the boat landing on the dock with a hollow thud. Clyde followed her but choose to stay outside of the house tracing Hitty's name on the ground with his shoe. He realized that if written just so the letters of Hitty could be read right side up or up side down making the word an ambigram.

All too quickly Maggie reappeared looking positively mournful. "**Lobster pots** and **Penobscot** barnacles! Hitty has moved to Sturbridge, Massachusetts!" she cried. "Oh, I'm mortified, dejected, in utter angst and pain that I've dragged us all across Maine."

Maggie's shoulders slumped. Wandering away and into a patch of **cranberry** vines she gently lifted the leaves to peek at the cranberries still tiny and looking more like green peas. Maggie felt rather tiny and green herself.

Page 18-19 Clyde allowed her a few moments of misery realizing that it is important to allow a little time for your feelings to run as long as you don't allow your feelings run you. Clearing his voice he said, "I'm reminded of our native son, **Henry Wadsworth Longfellow**'s words, 'The best thing one can do when it's raining is to let it rain'." For once Maggie was silent except for a little sniffling.

Being a gentleman, Clyde pulled out his handkerchief and pressed it into Maggie's hand then asked, "Would you please accompany me for a treat?" Maggie nodded still too despondent for conversation.

Page 20-21 The trip was unnervingly quiet. To lift her spirits Clyde motioned to Augusta as they passed by saying, "Won't you give your regards to the governor?" Maggie leaned into the wind and shouted, "Best wishes to our benevolent governor and grand **Augusta** our fair **Capitol**. We cannot stop stop today as we are on a quest."

With that Maggie sat back and eyed Clyde with curiosity asking, "Are we going for **Portland Lobster**? **The Holey Donut**? **Holey Cannoli**? **Wiscasset Treats**? **Red's Eats**? Clyde lifted a hand to quell the questions.

Page 22-23 Soon a quaint confectionary, the **Len Libby Chocolatier,** came into view. "One simply cannot go wrong with good chocolate," Maggie announced as she opened the door. "Just look at the turtles and truffles, bear, lobster and moose tracks. I see almond butter crunch, nibbles, pretzels and the delectable Maine Chocolate Bah in stacks." As Maggie turned she had such shock and delight that Clyde had to steady her for fear she would faint at the sight of **Lenny the Moose** staring straight at her. Standing eight feet tall and weighing 1700 pounds. Lenny observed Maggie unblinking from his chocolate pond. "I would like to introduce you to Lenny, Maine's most famous moose," Clyde said.

A tiny giggle bubbled up, followed by a chuckle, then a chortle and finally a side aching roar of laughter rang from Maggie. Once again being a good gentleman, Clyde offered his handkerchief so Maggie could wipe away her tears of joy.

Page 24-25 As they sat nibbling at chocolate moose antlers and lobster tails Maggie grew thoughtful again and said. "I wonder if there are caribou in Caribou?"

The end.

About The Author

Joyce R. Jackson is happily married to the extraordinary Dr. J. David Jackson. Currently they enjoy exploring New England, residing in Massachusetts after living coast to coast with New Orleans' mud between their toes during childhood. Her two beautiful daughters, Sarah and Rebekah are truth tellers helping people find sure footing. Her brilliant son Jonathan and his talented wife Emily improve the lives of everyone they touch including their puppies. These sweet people make the world a better place each in their unique way, and so should you.

About The Illustrator

Shaun Stotyn lives in Vermont with Monica, his wife, and his two children, Cadence and Ransom. He loves the outdoors, New England, and going to Maine every summer with his family.

Special thanks goes to:

Portland Lobster ©
180 Commercial St., Portland, Maine 04101

The Holey Donut ©
7 Exchange Street, Portland, Maine 04101

Holey Cannoli ©
72 Main Street
Waterville ME 04901

Wiscasset Treats ©
80 Main Street
Wiscasset, Maine 04578

Red's Eats ©
41 Water Street,
Wiscasset, Maine 04578

Len Libby Chocolatier ©
419 Blue Star Memorial Highway,
Scarborough, Maine 04074

Made in the USA
Lexington, KY
29 November 2019